The Wizard, the Fairy, and the Magic Chicken

Helen Lester
Illustrated by Lynn Munsinger

Houghton Mifflin Harcourt
Boston   New York

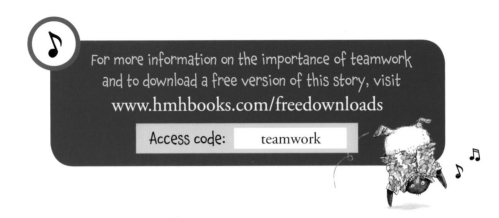

For more information on the importance of teamwork
and to download a free version of this story, visit
www.hmhbooks.com/freedownloads

Access code: teamwork

Text copyright © 1983 by Helen Lester
Illustrations copyright © 1983 by Lynn Munsinger

All rights reserved. Originally published in hardcover in the United States by Houghton Mifflin
Company, an imprint of Houghton Mifflin Harcourt Publishing Company, 1983.

www.hmhbooks.com

Library of Congress Cataloging in Publication Control Number 82-21302

ISBN 978-0-544-22064-5

Manufactured in China
SCP 10 9 8 7 6 5 4 3 2 1

4500461482

There once lived a Wizard, a Fairy, and a Magic Chicken.
Each thought, "I am the greatest in the world."
And each was very jealous of the other two.

"MY wand has a MOON on it," said the Wizard.

"MY wand has a STAR on it," said the Fairy.
"MY wand has a PICKLE on it,"
said the Magic Chicken.

"I can kiss a pig

and turn it into a bicycle," said the Wizard.

"That's nothing," said the Fairy. "*I* can kiss a bicycle and turn it into a bowl of soup."

"I can do better than that,"
said the Magic Chicken.
"*I* can kiss a bowl of soup
and turn it into a singing frog."

Each one always tried to outdo the others.

"I can make a hairy
monster with sharp teeth!"
bellowed the Wizard.

"*I* can make a bumpy monster with nine legs!"
screeched the Fairy.

"*I* can make a dotted monster with buggy eyes!"
yelled the Magic Chicken.

The monsters glared at the magicians and loudly said,

"GRRRRRROLPH!"

For the very first time the magicians agreed.

"RUN FOR YOUR LIVES!" they shouted.

"I will make a cloud to hide behind," gasped the Wizard,
but that didn't stop the monsters.

"I will make thunder to scare them," puffed the Fairy, but the monsters were not frightened.

"I will make lightning. That will make them go away,"
cried the Magic Chicken, but they would not go away.
Nothing worked.
"We'd better . . ." said the Wizard.
". . . try something . . ." said the Fairy.
". . . together!" said the Magic Chicken.

So they chanted, "One, two, three, *GO!*"
The cloud and the thunder and the lightning came together.
Suddenly it rained.

It rained so hard and the monsters got so wet that they shrank
until they were only very little monsters and
not scary at all.

"We did it!" cheered the Wizard, the Fairy, and the Magic Chicken.

"I must say, though," said the Wizard, "my cloud made the rain."

"Well," said the Fairy, "it was because of my thunder."

"But not without my lightning," said the Magic Chicken.

There once lived a Wizard, a Fairy, and a Magic Chicken.
They argued a lot,
but deep down they were very good friends.